The Singing Ringing Tree

Retold by Selina Hastings

Illustrated by Louise Brierley

Henry Holt and Company

NEW YORK

*T*here was once a Princess, famous for her beauty, who had been so spoiled by her doting father that she had grown vain and proud, thinking only of herself and demanding that her every wish be immediately fulfilled. So lovely was she that a man had only to look at her to fall in love. As a consequence she had received many offers of marriage, but had refused them all, considering no one worthy of her.

One day a Prince arrived at the palace. He had once from a distance caught sight of the Princess and had immediately lost his heart to her. Now he had come to ask for her hand. Kneeling humbly at her feet, he held out a casket of rare pearls – pearls as big as nectarines.

But the Princess looked with contempt at the Prince and his magnificent gift. She laughed at his proposal and overturned the open casket, scattering the priceless pearls in every direction on the marble floor.

"What do I want with you or with your casket of pearls?" she sneered. "Bring me the Singing Ringing Tree – then I will marry you!"

At these words the Prince bowed and turned sadly away. He had heard of the legendary Tree, whose leaves rang with music for those with love in their hearts; he knew, too, that to find it he must risk his life. But such was his devotion to the Princess that he did not hesitate. That very day he set off on his dangerous quest.

The Prince rode for many miles, through a dark forest and across a bleak and windy plain, until at last he entered a region full of strange boulders and bushes of cruel-looking thorns. There in a clearing stood the Singing Ringing Tree, its golden leaves shimmering in the sunlight.

The Prince eagerly dismounted, but before he could take a step towards the Tree, a tiny, misshapen creature leapt out at him from behind a rock. It was a hideous little manikin, with a big head, a small, hairy body, and legs which ended in pointy black hooves.

"Stay where you are!" it shrieked. "That Tree is mine! This is my domain and everything in it belongs to me!" Then the Dwarf narrowed his yellow eyes. "I know why you have come," he said, his voice soft with cunning. "You may take the Tree — but only on this condition: that if your Princess should refuse to marry you, then you and she must return here to spend the rest of your days in my power." He paused and his eyes glittered. "In my power — and in whatever form I choose!"

The Prince gave the Dwarf his word: he knew he had no choice. As he stooped to lift up the Singing Ringing Tree, its golden leaves, which had been motionless, began to quiver, and a sound as of a thousand silver bells rang out upon the air.

When the Prince arrived back at the palace, he once more knelt at the beautiful Princess's feet and held out the Tree to her. But the Princess behaved as ungraciously as before. Without a word of thanks she snatched the Tree from his hands. Now she had what she wanted. The fact that she had promised to marry the Prince meant nothing to her.

Running into the garden, she gave orders that the ornamental pool in front of the palace should at once be drained and the Tree planted in it. She gave not a thought to the fish that lay gasping and dying as the water ran away; and she failed to notice, as the Tree was put in place, that its leaves drooped and fell silent.

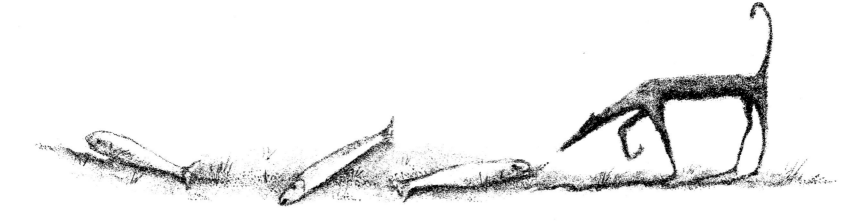

That night the Prince, his heart heavy with the knowledge that he was bound to return with the Princess to the Dwarf's domain, lay down beside the Tree and slept.

He was woken at first light by the sound of a woman sobbing: it was the Princess running distraught through the garden, her flawless beauty curdled overnight into a loathsome ugliness. At the same moment the Prince noticed to his horror that his hands were covered in thick brown fur. He had been transformed from a man into a bear!

The Dwarf's evil spell was already upon them.

Realizing that there was no escape from his terrible bargain, the Prince lumbered to his feet. Swiftly following the Princess, he threw her onto his back and galloped off with her mile after mile until he came to the nightmarish region in which the Dwarf lived.

The Dwarf was fiendishly delighted to have in his power the Bear-Prince and the
ugly Princess, and he hopped and danced about the wretched pair, cackling in triumph.
The Princess, overcome with misery at the loss of her beauty, was able to do nothing
but lie on the ground and weep. But the Bear, having tried to comfort her
as best he could, at once went about building a shelter
to protect her from the elements.

In the days that followed, the patient Bear worked ceaselessly to make the Princess's lot less harsh, bringing her fruit and nuts to eat and making a soft bed of moss for her to sleep on. Every night he lay on the hard ground outside the shelter to guard her from intruders. Gradually, through her wretchedness, the Princess began to notice the Bear's unfailing kindness, and how the animals and birds seemed to trust this big, ungainly creature—while from her they crept away in fear.

As the weeks passed, the Princess began to think a little less of her own plight and appearance. She even started to help the Bear gather food for them both.

One day, while alone looking for berries, she came across a unicorn with its horn caught fast in a thornbush. Its eyes were wide with fear and its head and neck torn and bleeding. Gently approaching, the Princess disentangled the poor creature, tearing strips off the heavy silk of her dress with which to bind its wounds.
It was the first unselfish action of her life.

The Dwarf was enraged by the Princess's show of compassion, knowing that if she were to learn how to love, his hold over her would be broken. Frowning with fury, he muttered the words of a spell. Immediately a terrible cold fell on his land. The ground froze hard as granite and the water turned to ice.

Half-perished, the Princess made her way back towards the shelter where she hoped to find the Bear. But on the way she passed a pond, frozen solid, in which an enormous fish was trapped and near to death. Moved to pity, she knelt on the bank and broke the ice with her bare hands so that the fish could swim free.

The Dwarf was now in a frenzy of rage. He stamped his foot, and instantly the captives' little shelter collapsed on the ground. With a pang of fear the Princess thought of the Bear: he might be in danger, and now for the first time she knew she loved him. She must find him and go to him at once.

But the Dwarf was determined to stop her. Again he stamped his foot, and a great torrent of water came gushing out of the earth in which the Princess must surely drown. But just as the water closed over her head, she felt the giant fish glide beneath her and swim her to safety.

Then the Dwarf raised both arms above his head, and a wall of flame roared up in front of the Princess. But at the same moment the unicorn appeared by her side. She climbed quickly on its back and, light as a bird, it soared over the fire.

There, on the other side of the flames, stood the Bear. Stopping only to thank the unicorn for saving her life, the Princess ran to him. She threw her arms about him and, in words that now poured freely from an unlocked heart, told him how much she loved him.

Even as she spoke, the spell was broken: the ground opened to swallow up the wicked Dwarf; the Bear once more regained his human form; and the Princess became as beautiful as before.

And as the two lovers made their way back to the palace, through the clear air they heard the silvery music of the Singing Ringing Tree.